the Continuing Saga of

Rikki Tikki Tavi

LaDene M. Hayes

Reading Glass Books
1-800-608-6550
www.readingglassbooks.com
production@readingglassbooks.com

Author LaDene M. Hayes suggests that you either watch the animation of "Rikki Tikki Tavi," created by Chuck Jones Productions or delve into the original story penned by Rudyard Kipling. This will provide you with a comprehensive understanding of why this serves as a seamless continuation.

Dedications

I dedicate this book to my former 7th grade students at Jackson Middle School who remember me as Ms. Clark and wanted to know what happened to the egg also.

I dedicate this book to my son, Xavier, and grandchildren, Xavier II and Danielle, who loved the animated cartoon Rikki Tikki Tavi.

I dedicate this book to my church family, The Christian Life Center of Greensboro, representing Bishop Joseph and First Lady Arnetta Gardner. All of you have been so supportive with your love and caring and tears and prayers. I can never thank you enough!

Acknowledgements

I would like to acknowledge my Lord and Savior, Jesus Christ, for all the good things He has done for me. Without Him, I am nothing.

I would like to acknowledge my sister, Vivian Hughes, for all her encouragement and motivation. I don't think she realized just how much I valued her opinions and ideas. Thanks, sis!

I would like to acknowledge Tate Publishing. When it comes to them, I am left speechless.

I would like to acknowledge my second grade teacher, Mrs. Ruth McRae. Had it not been for her, I never would have met Rikki Tikki Tavi. Thank you, Mom Ruth!

I would like to acknowledge the people that proofread my manuscript for me with nary a grumble, Mrs. Wyonia Davis, my sister, and my friends, Fred and Leigh Anne Hall. Thank you guys so much!

As a child, I recall spending hours reading and re-reading the story of Rikki Tikki Tavi. What a hero he was! His story was one that never lost its allure or magic for me.

Author LaDene Hayes (aka "Deanie"), like me, was also mesmerized by Rikki Tikki Tavi. She, however, chose to revive the Tavi adventure with *The Continuing Saga of Rikki Tikki Tavi* for the enjoyment of today's youth and parents as well.

The Continuing Saga of Rikki Tikki Tavi will make you cheer and praise the little mongoose that knew no fear! You will hold your breath as you read and visualize Rikki in action! I think your children will beg you to read and re-read *The Continuing Saga of Rikki Tikki Tavi* over and over again, as I feel your family will enjoy the Rikki Tikki Tavi experience for years to come.

So, thank you Sis, Deanie, Author Hayes, for creating this new Rikki Tikki Tavi saga for all families across America who remembered Rikki Tikki Tavi!

Vivian N. Hughes
Your Big Sis

Rikki was everybody's hero. He was pulled into Nag's den in the final battle with Nagaena and emerged victorious. Rikki killed Nagaena and destroyed the last remaining egg . . . or so everyone thought.

Two years have passed, and this is
The Continuing Saga of Rikki Tikki Tavi.

Part I

Rikki and the Rumor

It was the morning after a torrential downpour that Rikki Tikki began his survey of the gardens and surrounding land. He had his usual breakfast of soft-boiled egg and banana at the table with Adam and his wife, Bethany, and son, Lawrence, before starting his tour. Rikki knew it was important to stay slim, swift, and ready for the unexpected.

In the two years that Rikki had come to live at the bungalow, he had killed Karait, the brown death, Nag, Nagaena, their eggs, and seven deadly snakes, although none so dangerous and famous as the battle with the king cobras Nag and his wife. His fame and name were spread throughout the country by every flying creature far and wide. They sang of his courage and eyes of flame, "Rikki Tikki, stay away from him. When his eyes are flames, he will kill you dead!" Of course, Rikki ignored all the fuss because he knew that mongooses were supposed to fight and kill snakes. However, as much as he ignored their praises,

he could not ignore the fact that the relatives of the snakes he had killed were constantly planning to destroy him. Rikki had to stay ever vigil. As Rikki was touring the grounds, an agitated Darzi flew over his head and landed on a branch.

"Rikki! Rikki Tikki!"

"Rikki Tikki Tavi! Listen to what I have to say!" Darzi whispered excitedly to a slightly impatient Rikki.

"Yes? Yes? What is it? Hurry, Darzi. I must be on my way. What? What? What?" Rikki stomped his foot with emphasis.

"Rikki, Chuchundra told me that his cousin, Otis, was awakened one night to whispering voices saying that the brother of Nag declared that whoever kills Rikki Tikki Tavi and his masters will rule the big house and gardens forever. He claimed that Nagaena was moving her eggs to his den for safekeeping when Nag was killed. She was able to transfer only one before she had to fight you. He claims he has raised the child of Nag for two years now, and the death of Rikki Tikki Tavi is soon to come!"

The garden suddenly grew still. Rikki Tikki's eyes began to burn red.

The hairs stood up the length of his back as his teeth began to click, click, click. "Tik! Tik! Tik!" Rikki chattered loudly. "So, Nagaena hid one of her eggs with Nag's brother, and they want me dead. Well, we will see about that!" and off he dashed to find Chuchundra to verify what Darzi had said.

As Rikki searched for Chuchundra, he noticed a tiny heap of wet fur on the trail and stopped for a closer look. It was another mongoose! Was it dead or alive? Rikki inched closer and stopped when it moved.

Now what? thought Rikki. It rolled over, and the movement forced water from its mouth allowing a huge gulp of air to be inhaled.

"Ahhhhh," the mongoose exhaled and sat up slowly, coming face to face with Rikki.

Why, it's a girl,
Rikki said to himself.

A closer inspection revealed a very pretty one at that.

Rikki bristled. "Who are you? What is your name? How did you come to be here? Tell me quickly, or I shall bite you!" Rikki insisted threateningly, clicking his teeth for emphasis.

Part II

Rachel

Feeling the rush of air pour into her lungs caused a huge sigh of relief to escape her pale lips as the mongoose weakly and softly replied, "I do not remember my name or where I came from or where 'here' is. You may kill me if you wish, for I am too weak to fight and am trespassing on your property." Having said that, she went limp and slumped to the ground.

"Stay still," Rikki said, "I shall get help," and off he dashed towards the bungalow. Rikki managed to get Adam to follow him into the garden to discover the mongoose. Adam went back to get a basket to transport her in. Adam and his family were delighted and pleased to have two mongooses to care for them now.

Rikki did not care for all the fuss and watched from a distance, but he remembered his mission to find Chuchundra and resumed his search. Rikki found him quickly and verified that what Darzi had said was true. Nag's daughter lived!

Her name was Lethalee. She lived in a den a little distance west of the bungalow. She had a birthmark of a bright yellow fang on the edge of her lip. Matters worsened when Chuchundra revealed that she was about to lay her first clutch of eggs, but where, no one knew ... not even her uncle! This news thoroughly vexed Rikki. Not only did he have to find and destroy Lethalee before she laid her eggs; he had to deal with a beautiful and homeless mongoose with amnesia! Rikki had no experience in such matters but decided it was time for him to

learn. Throughout his life, Rikki had depended on his instincts to help him and decided this was no different. Whatever his first instinct would be about her, he would heed, and that would be the end of that. He headed for the bungalow.

Meanwhile, at the bungalow, the mongoose had been dried, fed, enveloped in a bed of soft cotton to warm up, and was sleeping peacefully. However, the strange surroundings did not allow her to sleep deeply because she came to a quick alertness at the sound of cautious rustling as Rikki Tikki approached.

Adam and his family apprehensively watched Rikki wondering how he would react to another mongoose, especially a beautiful female such as this one. They knew mongooses were territorial, possessive, and fiercely protective, but also family oriented. They wondered if Rikki would reject or accept this new mongoose, and knew that whatever Rikki decided, they had to honor it. The moment had come.

What would Rikki Tikki do?

She wasn't his responsibility. Adam, his family, the garden, and surrounding land were his responsibility. Rikki's mind was racing, trying to figure out what to do as he looked into the soft gray eyes of the mongoose. Her eyes held his boldly for a time before lowering to indicate willful submission. Instantly, Rikki knew he wanted her to stay.

Whispering in her ear, he said, "You may stay, and I shall call you Rachel." Raising her eyes to his and tilting her head slightly, she slowly smiled, showing acceptance.

"Thank you," she said. "I like my name."

As Rikki turned to leave, he heard Rachel say, "And by the way . . . what is yours?" Rikki turned and simply said, "Rikki." Rachel closed her eyes and began drifting back to sleep as Rikki heard her faintly say, "I like your name too." From that day on Rachel belonged to Adam, his family, and Rikki Tikki Tavi.

The family continued to nurse Rachel. During her convalescence, Rikki helped her exercise by taking her with him when he did his daily duties. She was getting stronger and stronger every day, and Rikki knew that with each passing day she was becoming more and more special to him.

Finally, the day came when he showed her the gardens and all the land he protected. He introduced her to the inhabitants of the garden and showed her where each one lived. He even showed her the place where he had fought and killed Nag, as well as the den of the final battle with Nagaena, which had been filled with dirt and closed up. He showed her the melon bed where he had destroyed the cobra eggs and the different hideouts of the snakes he had killed. Rikki shared all these things with Rachel . . . all except the news about Lethalee, which was constantly on his mind.

One particular day while Rikki was still showing Rachel the grounds, he was thinking about the day when he would have to face this new danger. It was more important than ever to find Lethalee, especially before she laid her eggs. That would be Rikki's first priority. The lineage had to be destroyed with Lethalee!

How can I find her?

What can I do?

I must hurry before time runs out,

Rikki thought to himself.

Part III

The Fight

"Rikki! Rikki! Help! "

It was Rachel! He had been so distracted in his thoughts that he had forgotten all about her and raced towards the sound of her voice. Not far ahead he came to a screeching halt. What he saw chilled his body and put fire in his blood at the same time! Rachel was surrounded by two king cobras poised to strike at any minute. He did not know if she was able to handle one cobra, much less two, and he had to be careful, quick, and precise. Rikki had never dealt with more than one snake at a time himself, so he was taking a great chance in assuming that Rachel was ready for a fight of such magnitude. No time to delay. The cobras were closing in fast, and Rikki had to move faster! He could only pray that Rachel would snap out of it and remember that she was a mongoose born to fight and kill snakes.

Rikki walked a wide circle around the cobras and chattered loudly to get their attention. His fur bristled and his eyes burned a blood red. "Tik! Tik! Tik!" clicked Rikki's sharp, white teeth. Clicking his teeth loudly and eyeing the cobra nearest Rachel, Rikki darted through the air just as the cobra drew back and swung around.

Rikki landed side by side with Rachel, and they were soon back-to-back. Rachel seemed to draw from his strength and stood up on her hind legs ready to face the challenge with him. It was now two against two! Rikki did not feel the need to coach Rachel because somehow, he knew she was ready, willing, and able. The fight began!

Almost simultaneously, Rikki and Rachel began bobbing up and down, looking for an opportune time to strike. The cobras bobbed and weaved to keep them off guard and away from their hoods.

Rikki suddenly had an idea. "Rachel," he whispered, "when the cobras strike, we will jump into the air, flip to the opposite side, and go for the head of the cobra furthest away from us. They will expect us to come head-on, not cross pattern, and by the time they realize what we have done, it will be too late."

Rachel shifted her weight against Rikki's back to let him know she heard him and braced herself for the attack. Rachel felt Rikki tense against her back, and she pressed into him for assurance. Together, they held that pose, watching each cobra.

With a hiss of their tongues and snap of their heads, the cobras lunged towards the mongooses. As fast as lightening strikes, Rikki and Rachel's leg muscles uncoiled, shooting them high into the air and propelling them into a flip. They crossed each other and landed feet first on the heads of the cobras, placing them in perfect striking positions. Their sharp white teeth bit deep into the heads just above the hood, and they held on for dear life!

A total of twelve feet of death writhed, rolled, and whipped, tossing the two mongooses fiercely, trying to dislodge the securely attached teeth of Rikki and Rachel. The battle seemed to rage for hours, carrying them deep into the tall grass.

Suddenly, the garden grew quiet. The dust settled, and all the animals of the garden seemed to exhale when they watched the tall grass part and reveal the figures of Rikki and Rachel dragging the dead bodies of the cobras.

"Hooray for Rikki! Hooray for Rachel! The mightiest, and the mighty times two!" sang Darzi and all the animals of the garden.

Rikki sneezed.

Adam had arrived with his gun, but the battle had already been won.

Part IV

The Secret

Oh, those silly birds, Rikki thought to himself. Rachel, on the other hand, felt very pleased from all the attention and excitement and smiled broadly at Darzi. Still excited from the battle, Rachel turned to congratulate Rikki only to see him staring at the dead cobras.

What's bothering Rikki? she thought as she looked from the snakes to Rikki and back again.

Rikki's eyes of flame fixed crazily on the face of one of the cobras. He began his battle dance and cry of rage again.

But the battle is over, thought Rachel. *What is exciting him so?*

"Rikki! Rikki! What is it?" asked Rachel with a little hesitancy in her voice. Rikki seemed to be hypnotized by the dead cobras and continued his dance of rage until he collapsed in an exhausted heap.

Without approaching him, Rachel asked again, "What is it, Rikki?" At the sound of her worried voice, Rikki seemed to pull himself back to the present and tried to compose himself. He could not tell Rachel that he recognized the birthmark of the Nag family on one of the dead cobras!

Oh, what a dilemma this is! thought Rikki.

With rage spent and head cleared, he turned to look at Rachel, careful to mask his shocking discovery.

How lovely she looks. How strong and beautiful and caring she is, thought Rikki. At that moment Rikki's heart exploded with love, and he was overcome to the point of tears! He didn't realize how much he loved her until then and knew instantly what he had to do.

Without hesitation, Rikki bowed to Rachel humbly with tears in his eyes and said, "Rachel, I should have done this the moment I was sure. I know now that I love you, and I want you to be my wife. Will you marry me?"

Rachel, eyes welling up in tears and at a loss for words, could only nod her head yes. Rikki kissed her the way a mongoose kisses and dashed off to make arrangements to be married in the garden that evening.

All the inhabitants of the garden witnessed the marriage of Rikki and Rachel. As the sun set, Rikki and Rachel watched it disappear as husband and wife.

Several months later, Rachel increased Rikki's happiness by telling him he was going to be a daddy.

However, that happiness diminished as Rikki thought about what Lethalee would do once she found out. Rikki knew that his family and he would never be safe as long as Lethalee lived!

As Rachel slept,

Rikki crept quietly outside to look at the stars and plan his next move.